This book belongs to:

Today something VERY VERY exciting happened!

Can you guess what it was?

We got a BRAND NEW BABY!

So now I am a BIG sister.

Mommy and Daddy said that being a
big sister is very special.

Our new baby is really small.

It has little hands, little feet and a tiny nose.

Our baby likes to sleep a lot...

Mommy and Daddy say that our new baby is too small to play with me yet, but that I can help take care of them because BIG sisters have an important job to do.

So far I have learned that our new baby likes to drink milk.

Our baby also likes to be wrapped up warm and cosy when they sleep.

I have watched Mommy and Daddy change our new baby's bum; it's very very smelly!

Mommy says they did this for me when I was little.

Daddy says that our new baby can't use the big girl toilet like me yet.

But when they get a bit older I can help to teach them how it works.

Lots of our family and friends have come round to see our new baby.

I like to show our baby off to them; everyone agrees our baby is adorable.

We look at pictures of when I was little like our baby is now. Everyone says that we look alike.
I don't remember being that small!

Mommy and Daddy get very tired now we have our new baby, they say the baby stops them sleeping at night.

Because I'm a BIG sister now I sometimes help Mommy and Daddy read our baby a story.

Our baby watches me and we look at the pictures together.

We both like the bright colourful pictures the best.

Sometimes our new baby cries.

Mommy and Daddy say this is what little babies do because they can not talk.

Sometimes it means they are hungry.

Sometimes it means they are tired.

I showed our new baby to my friends.

Some of them are important BIG Sisters too, just like me.

They all agree its Cool being a BIG Sister.

BIG Sister Team

When our baby gets bigger I will be able to show them some of my favourite things to eat.

Like Pizza and Chocolate. And vegetables - Mommy says fruit and vegetables help keep me healthy so I will grow to be big and strong.

Mommy and Daddy have showed me how to be gentle with our new baby.

Because they are so small and new we have to be very careful, but we can still hold them and give them lots of hugs and kisses.

I can share all my toys with our new baby too.

Because I'm now a BIG Sister it's important to share, and it's much more fun than playing on your own.

Even though Mommy and Daddy have to take care of our baby they still have lots of time to play with me.

And we still do my favourite things like playing in the park and eating ice cream.

Mommy and Daddy say that when our baby grows a bit they can join in and then it will be <u>even more fun!</u>

I love being a BIG Sister, it's the best job in the world.

The End

Titles also available on  by:
R.L Meadows

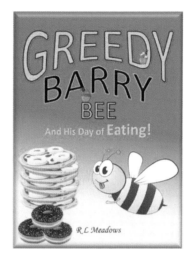

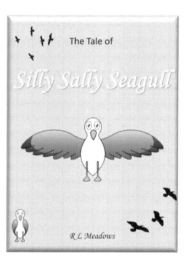

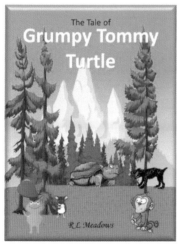

You Can Also Follow Us On:

 @r.l__meadows

 @rlmeadowsauthor

Printed in Great Britain
by Amazon

30305289R00016